I0749582

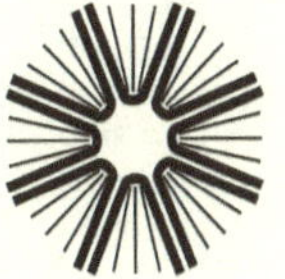

LETTER TO PETYA DUBAROVA

Letter to Petya Dubarova

Abigail George

GAZEBO BOOKS SUMMER HILL 2022

Gazebo Books
PO Box 375
Summer Hill
New South Wales 2130
Australia
gazebobooks.com.au

First published 2022

National Library of Australia
Cataloguing-in-Publication Entry
George, Abigail, 1979– .
First edition
ISBN 978 0 6454648 2 5

Cover and interior design by Mountains Brown Press.
Cover and frontispiece image: Philippa Riddiford, *Turn Around* (2020), archival giclee printed onto 310 gsm matte cotton rag paper, 59.4 cm x 84.1 cm. Courtesy of the artist.
philippariddiford.com

You grew up in Burgas. I grew up in Port Elizabeth. By the sea bustling with bluebottles every January. This is a kind of lamentation for thunder, manifestos, and my father the king-man, the Parisian rooftops of Picasso and Modigliani, Rilke, Hemingway and Salinger. Petya Dubarova, I say your name like we're friends or something. Like we went to school together, had sleepovers. Stuff. Shared our poetry with each other like homework instructions. The only thing that we have in common is that we are two female poets. I have known the experience of death in the asylum. Family pain. Philosophy poured out into verse. The exquisite fire-red lipstick of my sister. Dream and poetry. The words of Abigail George are words oblivious to empty love. The other truth. Diary of a poet. Of a misfit. My fragile mind, how those words ring inside my head like the tune of a Roman wedding. Women poets meet the light and the darkness. Poetry will never feed you, but it fed the plays of Sarah Kane. Giorgio Manganelli, Salvatore Quasimodo and Pier Paolo Pasolini. Alda Merini. And me. That hand to God. Love me or kill me. The voice is all. The lonely victory. I say to it, come on out and join the dance. Grotesque and curious is the spider's web. My childhood was a web too. Isolated, the enterprise of impoverished loneliness. I have a secret brain disease, a disordered female brain. But there is no male nor female mind. No dominant sex when it comes to poets.

I think of your Burgas, Petya. Your sea. Behind the walls of the big house, you will find the sea and me. Both deceived by youth and forgiveness, sleep and memory. The sea and I have known restoration through therapists. The gold dust of lithium therapy. Gone am I with the rainy season, domesticity, sketches in pen scratches, liberty, elders, and the sick poetess. My father uses a walker. My mother drives the car. I have had two relapses this year already, April and October. I go to the sea. Walk on the beach amongst the black ghosts dressed in the costume of breaking code. Think of being kissed by the sea. I see normal people. They see me. My sister is a normal girl. My mother was a normal girl. I am anti-normal. Anti-muse.

I think of Brighton. Think of every female poet who has ever thought of committing suicide. Think of my four attempts, of how it felt the first time, then the second, then the third, then the fourth. This kind of fragility in me. In imperfect and random me you will find the things you love. Flowers and roots and stems and sap. I am the sap you spat out. I am replaced by other women's daughters. The magic salt saved my life. Afrikaner psychiatrists. There's something wrong with me. Guess everyone can tell. There's something wrong with me inside. Guess my heart is broken from all of those years of trauma. You love me. Then you don't. You accept me. Then you don't. I think of desire. Then I don't. I write. That's what I have always done. Like it is a form of revenge or something. They say like daughter like father. That I am just as crazy as him. Just as lunatic. Just as black a sheep. Just as burnt out from life. If I could smoke my life away, believe me I would. If I could drink my life away, believe me I would, if I were so inclined. I am a poet gone mad. You're all of me, Dad, and I'm all of what you are. I think I know what I am. The psychosocial action of the black vein in a leaf. I think of stigma and discrimination. The dynamic that exists between mother and daughter. The mother is the winner standing in the middle of the gap. Her daughter is miserable. She's failed at having children and spouse. I'll turn into an island, you'll see. I think of you, Mother, as I do of the flowers in your garden. How like them you are. How filled with focus and concentration you are, hip-deep in your work. You're rather something special, made of vital poetic substance. I wish you could love me the way I love you, be proud of me the way I am proud of you. I'll turn into a bird, you'll see. I'm ink catching a fish catching a genius, and the owl screams while the bat twitches and the mole snitches, and the moonlight is zen.

Zen. Tonight, I'm thinking of my paternal grandfather. I'm thinking of his smarts, his tattoos, his children, his alcoholism, his baptism, his restoration, and how I flesh him out now in words. How he spoke the language of the Second World War. How he was a cold sea, a waking child in the middle of the night. How much I loved him. How much I'll always love him in the big night's dark grasses, and mountain air. The valley of it all razed with guns and bullets. All the people I have loved are gone, or dead. Flung all over the world. Never to return to me. America, Berlin, Swaziland, Johannesburg. They all tell me how difficult it is to love me, my madness-life, from the glass ceiling to the chandeliers. It is difficult to love someone like me, they say. I'm in the cold sea too. I'm from Bulgaria. I'm from Africa. I live within a hemisphere of social isolation, fear and anxiety, and stars like fireworks inside the cellular network of every nerve fibre of my brain. You're perfect, Grandfather. I'm rebellious. Your other granddaughter had a Berlin Christmas. I've turned into an island, you see. You're abundant, Grandfather. In everything I do, I see, I know, I acknowledge, I write. You're still attached to me like a wishbone. You stand in solemn mode armed with a bayonet. Then, saint, you're home with five mouths to feed. I never went to university. You never went to university. I never finished school. All I ever wanted to be was a poet and an editor, like Ezra Pound. An admirer of Pound's Alba and Sappho, Antigone and Joan of Arc. Mother Teresa of Calcutta. And the island's name is Saint Helena.

If you're a flower, Mother, then so am I. If you're summer, good-looking, then I am winter's bulbs stuck in earth by gravity. I am third-eye wiser. I am the wheel, the spark. I am lonely. I am both alone and lonely in this world of ours. With one light on, I know you are a home mother. With one foot upon the stair, wind in your hair, you are an angelic flame. You, like my grandfather, are a saint. You're the axis, the planets, the stars, the sunlight.

You're the riot of the phantom thread, the golden thread of this planet, the rollercoaster machinery of Monkey Island, the theme park of Africa, the aloof poetess of Bulgaria. I am mulatto. You, Petya, are as pale as milk. Hair as thick as molasses. The colour of honey. I did not smile in photographs either when I was your age. Even in death, frozen in time you bloom at specific will. With the focus, growth-process, the speed of a flower. Like a wildflower. Like all wildflowers. I am so pale. The colour of death. Down into the yards of the grave of the sea I must go. Book passage there. Rooms made of star signs and water, silence and music, the hours. Don't look down there into the abyss, I told myself.

I knew of love once. He gave me *National Geographic* magazines to read. He's long gone to the States now. I know he'll make a roaring success of himself in the image of Fitzgerald. Thought he'd be perfect for me. Thought I'd be perfect for him. He pulled me up from the funeral waters to his heart. I was alive again. We lived for each other, Petya. Then the day came when we had to say goodbye. The moon sat above the silent streets that night when the moonlight left my soul. Dove warbling in my throat talks across the page. My heart is lonely again. My head is a foolish wasteland of cowardice and fear, my heart is a cage, all I can think of is the pain of this relationship. We'll both be estranged for the rest of our lives. He'll fall in love with another, I know this. But I want him right now and this room spins. My heart wants to scream out loud. I'm always falling, tumbling down, rambling, falling like a leaf to a shroud, like vapour from a cloud. I'm always falling in love. I haven't been very successful at it. The love affair is wasted on me. I can see no potential in it. It makes me feel empty inside. I want to be more than a grain of sand. The tears are always falling. Petya, did you know love in your short life? Aspire to it? It feels so empty without him here now. The music, the hours, the silence, the water that I slipped into for my baptism. I was baptised in the local swimming pool by an apostle. Life feels so empty. Petya, could you and I have been intimate friends? Shared everything, everything. All I can think about is this guy. I wish he was still around to make me laugh. America is like another constellation.

If you wanted to be found, we could have found each other. If I wanted to be found, you could have found me. When I dance, I hope you're coming for me, but you don't. You don't see my grace. You don't see the way that I see the sea. It hurt so much to let you go. To see you standing there for the last time. For you, I'm the hungry lioness. I'm a carcass that wild birds feast and claw their way upon. All I can think of is you. But you're gone. Gone to America. You can do anything you want with this heart of mine. Loving you has only caused me pain. The wound will never heal, it feels like. You're leaving town. I'm left hanging around. How sweet it was to call your name, how sweet it was to know desire, how sweet it was to have you in my life, call you friend, call you love. I have known others. In a way they're dead to me now, they've moved on. Onward. Where did you go, where am I going, after this? That sunny road will always be so incomplete. Nothing I can do about the pain. You're not here. You're a pale king on your throne. I'm just a poor girl, impoverished and lonely. Call it a secret then. Call it desire.

Your Monkey Island, Petya, has become mine. So, I live to survive, to fight another day. I live to write. That's part of my deception. That was part of your deception too, Petya. He was a young king. My sister is in Berlin. It is raining there. I long for your Bulgaria to kiss this pain away. I long for my Africa to kiss this pain away. I keep waiting for the telephone to ring long distance. Hear the sound of their voices again. But it is just a hallucination. Part of my personality type now, to hear voices. There are no voices now. Only goodbye. He's gone. The music has stopped playing. All I see now are false people around me, haunting me with the triumphs of their ghost nation, with their falsities, or their niceties. And sometimes even their loneliness, their false bravado, their libretti written on their chests. All I wanted was to love, and be loved in return, and for a short while I was. He was too. Gone, only to be forgotten. Gone, forever and a day, until the hours to the next sunset. In return for his silence, he gets mine, Petya. I think of Burgas this time of year. Could it be summer where you are, where your bones are, where your poetry is? For my entire life I have worn a mask, Petya. I've experienced trials in living, in loving, in writing. For me, the world has been wintertime. Help me live, Petya. Please, help me. Behind me is the northern star of the death wish. Make it go away, I tell my identity. I am through with it. I have known so little love in my short life. No view of the world. No view of the bride. No view of the groom. I am shy of the world, of the universe. There is nothing left in it for me, except to drown in its waterfall. Pull myself away from the current phase in my life. This relapse into the doll-like flowers of winter. Leaves in a hat. Do not touch it. Leave it behind. Tithe in the collection plate. Leave it there to always mark my father's place. Petya, you're magical, funny and truly soulful. Petya, your poetry is classical, timeless, and a must-see. I am uncut, un-magical, un-funny, not soulful. For if I were soulful, Petya, then wouldn't someone fall in love with my soul?

I am Japan from memory, from memes, from verse, from rhyme. I am a diarist. I am an insomniac. I am lovesick and want to be seduced. I am old. I am older. You will always be young. You will always be younger. In my estimation all female poets are wise at any age. I will not read about the male poets anymore. Except Nick Laird. I really dig Nick Laird's poetry. His wife's novels. I've read Updike. Read Hemingway. Read Salinger. There was a time when I wanted everything. Then came a time when I only wanted the pursuit of happiness. Now all I want is to be truly happy, exposed as poet.

Everyone who marries meets at university. I think of you all the time, with love, with respect, with admiration. Why am I so sad? I lost the love of my life again. It feels as if I'm in my twenties again. You with the sad eyes, what am I going to do with you? You love, you love, you love and nobody loves you back. Her eyes look so sad. The reflection cast in tones, in silver, in speech and pause. The young king never loved me back. Inside I feel so sad and over-wrought. Ill. Ill. Ill. Yet still feminine and all I want to do is shine. Like you. Like you. Like you. I'm old. Too old for you. You're a prisoner. I'm a woman. You're leaving me. Father, brother, mother, sister. Greener pastures and the fairer sex await on the other side. I think of you smoking your last cigarette of the day. You're perfect. You're perfect just the way you are. I could glorify you in a handwritten poem. Kiss. Kiss. I could kiss you. Forgive you. Be in it for the long haul. You're in love, my love. You're leaving town. I'm swinging from the chandeliers. Burning the candle at both ends. Open your mouth and let me kiss you. You're thrilling and formidable. How come I've never found love. Don't want it. Don't need it. I'd rather partake in cheesecake. I think of you. I think of you all the time. I always have and I always will. Everything I have ever done, is done. And here I am writing again to you, David, my love. Always David. Always my love. And I will always be forever yours, but you are taken and someone else's dream man. She loves you. Go to her. This will be goodbye then. All I want to know is this. Did you love me, once? Afraid? Yes, I am afraid. I am scared of the dark, for example. All I want is you. You. You. But we are children of the … this is difficult to say … we are children of the revolution. We are children of the struggle. You know it. You know it. I know it. And all I can think of is being in your arms and loving you. Go to her. Go to your life partner. You made a commitment to her. Go. I've been in the wilderness for a long time. Half of Moses. You have your journey. You have your own journey. But do we meet again as friends, or lovers, or maybe nothing at all? I was always, even as a little girl, falling in love with father substitutes. I would tell them all I know. This would make them smile. I am a child of the revolution. And you? How I love you, David. How I love you, David. How I love you, David. How I love you, David. I will go on loving you for an eternity. Stay with me. Stay with me. Stay with me. I will adore, worship and love you forever. In the middle of the night I am the girl not in reach of anyone, except you. David, you are the only constant in my life. In the silence, which is as unbearable as the loneliness, the futility of always being the outsider looking in, David, is the only constant in my life. Ignore what everyone else says, and run away with me. Let's elope if this love has substance, and if this is for real. David, I only want to love you. David, David, David, David, take me away from all of this hell and fury, the misery that loves company, live with me and be my love. You, David, of all people understand what I think, what I feel, what I know, how I react to your voice. Is this hello or goodbye? I don't know yet. The decision is up to you, David. If you want me, I am here. I am waiting for you. I am waiting for love. Wait until I see your eyes again, that smile, that laugh. I look young enough again to be your daughter.

I don't care what other people say. I love you. How can I regret anything? You are yours. You are a man, and I am Eve. Hearts will be broken. I look at you and I see that you need someone who not only loves you but understands you completely. But you are not a free man, or, perhaps you are. I pray. I pray for you. Think of your silhouette in the dark. Think of you in the morning. I am all alone. I have always been all alone. You are my light in the dark. Whenever I think of you, I think of you as a lover, and a friend. You make me laugh. You make me want you. You make me want to be a kinder, more understanding woman. I love, love you. I adore you. I worship you. My life is just beginning. Yours? Tell me, how are you? Are you loved? Can't get your name out of my head. You make me forget my dreams. I only want to dream them with you. I pull the hair back from my face. Holding my hair up with bobby pins. I dance for you, and then suddenly I'm in love, and all I can think of is you. How imperfect you are. I am too. How perfect you look. Even after all these years you still look the same to me. You're the music inside my head. The love song inside my head. Joy Division in the background. Remember when I was working as a cocktail waitress in the bar where we met? Are you nothing but a careless whisper?

A heart-shaped bullet passing straight through me. Nothing but yesterday. Words pass me by. Words pass me by now. Words are like bees. Words are like the mist. Words are like circles, shifting in the light of day. You were once given a chance. You were once an opportunity for a love affair and matters of the heart. I can only see my shadow now on the pavement in front of me, leading me home. My mother doesn't love me in the right way. She tries, like I tried to tell you once that perhaps I had feelings for you. Remember this. Remember. *Je me souviens*. You left me first. Standing there, looking at your gorgeous back as you walked away from me. I felt devastated, left. Empty, left. Left behind, left to fend for myself. It was a kind of omen for everything in my life. Go to your devoted wife. Your beautiful daughter you created together. My cold, cold heart was not undone by you, but by God. There've been so many loves over the years, my love, and all I can think of is one. For now. A novelist, a lecturer, a creative consultant, an educationalist, a producer, a researcher, a filmmaker, a clinical psychologist, a magistrate, and the list goes on. I know I have loved, I will love, and so forth. But I don't want to get all Coco Chanel over you, or Norma Jean Baker, or Britney Spears, or Kardashian. I don't just want to exist;

I also want to live. I want love. I want to love but I am terrified of it.

And so I write. I write to save, make a change, heal the world, heal myself. Always thinking of the novelist, always thinking of what could have been. Me, sixteen, with sad eyes. Time to grow up. Time for recovery and not relapse. Time to think, to mature, to remain confident. And all the girls are so, so pretty. And all the boys are so, so handsome. And all the good men have gone. All the women are married. All the handsome men are gay, so Robbie Williams sings. Nobody wants to kiss someone who has been raped. No one wants to know her name. The wedding dress is reserved for women who want to be lovers who turn into mothers. No one hears this woman sobbing into her pillow. Everyone ignores, has ignored, her pleas for help. So she thinks of her first loves, her second mother sleeping in the graveyard alongside Ingrid Jonker, she thinks of eddies of dust on the mountains in the pure greenness of Swaziland, and she thinks of her novelist. Always saying hello, goodbye. Reading women, the phoenix and somehow finding the exit. Petya, pain is the hardest thing. It's flippered. Like home, it has a soul, body, and mind of its own. It has the call of a swallow swallowing song, releasing the god of dew in the morning.

Darkness has come again. He has no face. He is faceless. He has been here again. Lenny Williams, my great-uncle. He has no face. Headless from where the rope around his neck separated his neck from the rest of his body. They cut him down from the rafters. I see him as an apparition. I think of the price of acceptance whenever disaster strikes in my world.

I think of home, or I go home. Home as sanctuary, a soft place to fall in flight and adrenaline rush. Welcomed by elderly parents, a happy dog licking my hand. An old man forgets everything. Daughters, though, have long memories. Memories of their wasted potential, and their mothers' wasted potential, memories of the tender eyes of the first high school boy they kissed, memories of painful things, memories of regret, and desire, and of wasted pain. I always thought of angels hiding in the dark ocean. Coming out into the light like volcano-lovers, or smoking and drinking like Hemingway and Fitzgerald in France. I thought of Sharon Olds, and Patricia Highsmith, oh, gosh, how much I wanted to be like them, how much did I want to enjoy sex, being kissed, pulled in close, held in a man's arms. But for most of my life, I was a blind oak, a sleeping woman, in pieces, in constellations, found in the galaxies of other worlds. I thought that marriage could save him pain, but it only illuminated my mother's. Sex was non-existent for her for years after my birth. I looked at her and wanted to be her. In control without antidepressants, or sleeping pills, sane with a man, sane without a man. There was something about her intuition that was divine, almost natural in the supernatural. Then there was her faith, her courage, the price she paid. I was raised in the household of a strong woman. Leaf falls to ground. Belief defies religious belief, norm becomes opinion, girls have fun, let loose at university, but I didn't. I lost myself in films and art exhibitions. The rain always caused a pensive transformation for me. For the sea I would dress in skinny jeans, comfortable sandals, and a t-shirt, if it was warm outside. It was always important to me how I looked to men first, and women second. All women were affectionate to me. My father always had self-destructive patterns in his behaviour. He used to drink, was popular with men, and women, dreamed himself up a bisexual persona. I had to live with him, my mother had to live with him.

Sunday mornings he was in church beside my mother, and my mother, ever protective of me, her only child, her only daughter, sheltered me from my father. Told me to grow up to be a radical, a feminist writer, a thinker. To be an intellectual. Nothing like her. She was a housewife, and sang in the church choir, sometimes taught Sunday School, the piano, and acted small parts in small plays sometimes, here and there. Always in a supporting role. She was a dreamer, everybody said so. Then they looked at me and said that I was just like her. We had the same large brown eyes, same hair, same dreams. I had to have goals, and plans. It made me forget about the time I found my father wearing pink lipstick and peacock-blue eyeshadow, sleeping it off. Summers meant holidays, hiking, and in my own writing it meant wilderness. Anything could be planted there, and it wasn't complicated, unlike my history with boys in high school. It made me feel complex, the writing one of my teachers said once, unfairly, was more quantity than quality. How I hated her for that, planned her death from a mugging and a gunshot wound to the head, and even planned my own death from an elixir of sleeping pills and whiskey. The bullets would be heart-shaped, and I'd be playing Russian roulette with a make-believe gun.

Now, I think of my mother, of her androgynous beauty so like my own, of what had attracted her in the first place to my father, that first sexual impulse, the first time he touched her. That was the catalyst for my own writing, touch. I remember my writing from childhood and adolescence, how dark it was, the colour of the day, the stolen blue in the middle of it, a sea of wave after wave that belonged to the ocean of my youth.

I remember the days I called you Simon, Jacob, Elijah, Nicolas, Patrick, or Benedict, or Ignatius, or someone else's name, that I just don't care to remember at all anymore. You're older, you're wiser, you left me innocent and sweet, but your romance was a sham. Love, so naïve, so trusting, so maybe it is for the long haul, maybe it's just a short-term plan, in the interim, while you wait for someone else to love you. I've been in the arms of poverty. Poverty is familiar to me. The world, my world, is tilting again. Shadows disappear. Shades appear in the gloom. You're like a fish. Here, and not here. There, and not there. Nature makes beautiful things. The flowers you don't buy, I buy for myself. The chocolates and wine you don't buy, I buy for myself. I want to make a tree out of you. Trees are cool. They help put a kind of fizz over the day. I feel myself falling, falling, falling. I'm exhausted. Think of the mad Zelda Fitzgerald who didn't like Hemingway's friendship with her husband, the exquisitely put together advertising genius Assia Wevill, think of Marilyn Monroe at the Actors Studio, wanting to become an 'actor', not just an actress flirting with the camera. I fall into the swell, the push-and-pull of night. I don't behave. The waves inside my head spill over into the day. The roots of grief, grief for the girl I once was and am no longer, are like balloons disappearing into the blue sky. The comfort of strangers is familiar to me too. One day, I wore a frock-dress, old-fashioned I know, with short sleeves, to the office. You told me that I looked beautiful. Took me in your arms. Non-reality is non-reality. I can't remember what we said to each other anymore. So much for the flame. I waltz in my bedroom, barefoot, dancing until I'm quite mad with joy, until my pupils are dilated as if I'm high, and I remember your kindness, and sometimes I even find somewhere I wrote your name down. You make me want to be a woman dressing up in men's clothing. Still smelling of girls, and booze on a Friday, and Saturday night. Your mouth fills with cigarette smoke, as you light cigarette after cigarette, playing the field, sowing your wild oats, a new girl in your bed every night. There's a new girl on your arm at a social gathering, or a work function. I've disappeared somewhere. I'm not walking down your street again. You never call. You never brighten up my day. We don't discuss the burning issues on the news. Your home was spirit-led, filled with prophetic talk, filled with brethren on a home visit on a Sunday, and in the deep dark night I would pretend I made you laugh. The smile would reach your eyes, you'd stroke my cheek, my bottom lip as if there was no tomorrow. Yes, I'm sick. They say it's my heart. Hearts can never be trusted. Hearts become lovesick over time.

Nicolas (there, I said it, I remember your name), tell it like there still is a maybe for us. After all this time, are you still sometimes afraid of the dark, do you sleep with the light on, the bedspread over your head? I dream. I dream of us. It's more or less an illusion. All I want to be doing is to be lying there, helpless in your arms. My name is Janice when I get angry, and low, trying to find the exit. You don't believe me. I'm just a ghost. I haunt, and haunt, and haunt, but I don't haunt you. I'm a bit of a joke to you. Sad, and melancholic, never reaching for anyone. I'm hungry for rumpus, for an extrovert to balance me out, and out, and out. I remember everything about you. You remember nothing about me. I look at myself in the mirror, standing there in the nude, before my bath. I tap my ribcage. I'm bone-thin now, but who's looking anyway in my direction? I'm older now. Wiser too. As wise as the language of blood spilling into test tubes every few months. I am as wise as this vein. All I do is eat yoghurt these days, and green salad. I get plenty of rest. I must get my rest. Whenever I get to Osage County to eat catfish, or Portland, or Maine for that matter, or Louisiana, I will keep whatever romantic feelings I have for you in my reading hands. There's a nervous energy here, calling to me. My waking lungs, my untitled passion for you, Nicolas. There are far-off branches floating like gulls in the fractured wind. If I had been beautiful the way an actress is beautiful, my skin as pale as milk, would you have loved me then? I am a brown girl.

If only you could see me now, Ouma, look at your 'great running leap for humankind'. I know, I don't make you proud, because I'm not beautiful. And a girl in the brown community, who didn't go to university, well, she must be beautiful if she is to be loved. Aunts felt sorry for me, cousins who were daughters, and the marrying kind, didn't feel anything for me. I was a reading woman, reading all the time.

My ex-lover is at work. I wonder who he is attracted to now, if he's fallen in love, who is the secret object of his affection, and I wonder what her name is, what she tastes like, smells like, moves like on the dance floor, sounds like in church, how she walks, how she talks on the exhale. Books always tasted of sea light to me, the thrilling cadences, and rhythms of borders, and salt, and air. That strange hissing sound as meat touched grease in the pan that hit the air, a woman's perfume like a risky adventure with an exciting, and tall, dark, and handsome stranger from an off-campus bar, sea air in my lungs, the vibrations of classical music reminding me of waves hitting the shoreline. Peak breaking, trough meeting trough, and light. The sea, like the kitchen table, was always sacred to me. I remembered Paul's words, but what could words do anyhow? She (he was talking about me) doesn't even know how to do sex, how to kiss even. That's not all she doesn't know how to do in bed. The guys guffawed. The guys cheered him on to tell them the whole story, the sob stories, the scenarios in the bedroom. He said, she said, the talk got louder, the conversation boisterous. I turned inward. My identity cemented in this crowd of strangers. What could intimacy between a guy and a girl possibly mean? He's infatuated with her looks, she's infatuated with the vision that he has of her. It is a lonely hunting-and-gathering game between the two parties. One searching for meaning and respect, the other a sign of devotion, admiration. And again, I turned inward, felt like an orphan from a country orphanage, self-pity rising up in me like an award for the role I was playing.

Am I too serious, Petya? What else is wrong with me besides stating the obvious? Am I following in my father's footsteps? Head on? When my father was sick to death and his world was coloured with pharmaceuticals, a pale sadness, he too went to the hospital for 'a rest'. My siblings and I played on the thin, grassy part of the garden at the clinic. Under neatly trimmed hedges and trees in Port Elizabeth, we watched our parents talking to each other in hushed tones. I will never forget those whispers the three of us were not supposed to hear. I, the little, impoverished bird, have improved now that my sister has gone away.

I no longer trail in your wake wondering what the ending to this drama is going to be. I can still smell your hair as if it were an elixir. I can feel your physical body's magical space where it left its warmth. You could not stop my flight into mania, me bolting into the blackest dark of futility and what was at the heart of me. I wanted you to possess all of me, see a picture of the hellish wasteland that I went through, but you wanted no part of that cut-out of the sea inside my head. Your silence from those years, the year you wrote the Matriculation exam still cuts through me. My territory has slowly but surely multiplied. Your journey as a goddess has finally ended.

I am a child again. I watch girls wearing swimsuits and bikinis and want to be older, grown up. I watch them as they tease their friends. The ones who seem like they cannot swim just put their feet in the water or sunbathe. Girls watching the boys, the boys watching the girls. My mother hisses at me to do something, to stop staring and why did I bring my doll to the beach. I am going to lose her, silly me. I have already lost the safe world that my brother and sister seem to inhabit. I am a nuisance, a pest, despised by the adults around me because I am a know-it-all. If my mother says these things to me, then other people, perhaps even children, must also be thinking it. I do not feel emotions now. It is becoming easier and easier to feel that way in my mother's presence. I can almost feel my heart in my chest. I do not feel the heat of the day anymore. Instead, just a pressure flooding through me that feels like I am on the verge of tears because her words are hurting me. They are pins and needles. The tears do not come. They do not have the guts to. I know that if I fail at that, it will mean the death of me. This is Massachusetts. Snow only comes in winter. Children and even the adults make snowballs and play in it on the news. I can feel beads of light behind my eyes. The soft, bewitching, pink mouth that parts in the grotto is not mine, curls soft to the touch do not belong to me. The young girls and boys that leave hollows behind in the sand this festive season I have nothing in common with (always, always, always). I watch girls as they 'disappear' with 'nice' boys at the beach as a child and wonder when it will be my turn. Nothing is hot. Not the sand, my bronzed skin, the towel sticky where the ice cream dripped off its stick, the white rays of the sun that seem to connect with every fibre, cell and fire of my child being. I see my mother's floppy hat and how she shields her eyes keeping her eyes on the waves. All I can think about was how pretty I am not. When I remember this, I imagine myself in love. Then I am brought to life by the familiarity of a fantasy life built, stored up extravagantly, in words.

Facts exist. This planet is hell. Men want the girl, and seldom want the woman. All girls want poetry in their lives. All women want is the large house and the kiddies but for her there is power in comfort and solitude. She found a hole in the sky to creep into. A blue cave, and this is where she wrote. Visionaries can see their reflections everywhere they look. She knew her escape from the drudgery of her work was that she had to love. That she had to live, think and act like a man to be an intellectual and a philosopher. One man told her that he didn't have the time of day for women who became overwhelmed by his terms or women who became emotional. He thought that was disgraceful behaviour. Fear and depression are examples of pain. All three are chronic. All three will lead you down the laws of Whitman's path. Are you witty, another man asked her. Are you scared of being with a real man? Are you innocent? There are always sides. Men who are dreamers. Men who have stories.

One man wanted to know what she did when he was not around. She answered honestly that she read a lot. I can see, he said. I can see you have many books. What kind of books do you read? Romance novels? She could hear the laughter in his voice. The smile in his voice. I read everything, she said in a small voice. Do you have anything to drink? No, she answered. I will leave you here with your books and I will pop out and get us something to drink. You look like you need a drink. He looked her up and down and smiled at her. You have beautiful hair. Do you always wear it like that? You should. It shows off your best features. Your high cheekbones. Your aquiline nose. The man started to stroke her face. Put loose strands of her hair behind her ear. You are a girl who understands intellectual life, and he smiled again but it was more of a smirk than a smile. You seem to be a girl who puts herself in a lot of dangerous situations, sweetheart. Not all men are like me but I think you know that already. I drink whisky, she said. No, he said. Today you are drinking what I drink. She stared up at him. Stared at his handsome face. Met his gaze and looked away again. Sweetheart, there are no good men. I am not good for you. The only thing a real man has is his personality. Character goes out the window when he is misbehaving. He closed the door behind him.

She got up from where she was sitting and looked out the window as he got into his fancy car. She hoped he was never coming back. That he would forget the number of her flat at the complex where she stayed. She wrote in her journal. I have often thought of what is beautiful and what is ugly in this world. What separates the truth of a man's character and personality? I have a wardrobe full of dresses to make me feel pretty. To make me feel extraordinary. To make me feel like an exceptional woman. (Thought of the meat defrosting on her kitchen table, the meal she was going to prepare with ground beef that evening. But the man, as usual, had other plans in mind.) Her father hadn't wanted her to go to the city. He had told her that she would not find herself there, nor her life purpose. He had asked her to stay. There was an urgency in his voice. Stay, please, Becky, but she was headstrong. She had made her decision.

The man was back. She could hear him walking up the stairs. He was whistling. He didn't knock, just walked right in as if he was certain that she didn't lock the door behind him. Party time. Are you ready for that drink now? I brought a friend with me. She is waiting downstairs for me in the car. Can she come up? At a loss for words, I see. Okay. Don't bother with glasses. This is how you entertain your friends, I assume. Your male friends. Get comfortable. Don't be shy. I don't think that women are shy creatures. You are more woman than girl to me. She looked at him. The man who had told her that he was a father and a husband. The man who had a wife and progeny. If only his children could see him now. Where are your children, she asked him in a quiet voice. I don't know, really. Visiting their grandparents. Your wife, she said, trying to keep her voice even, where is she? She travels a lot. Travels all over. I think she is landing in Cape Town as we speak, but enough about them. What about you, little woman? You have a body on you. Still going to make me supper? Are you sure my friend can't come up? She must be bored by now thinking where in the world I am. I promise she won't bite. Have you ever been with a woman before? I think everything about you is erotic. He opened the bottle, leaving the silver foil and the cork on the floor and began to drink straight from the bottle, gutturally. A little bit of erotica never hurt anyone. You have gone all quiet on me now, woman. Am I shocking you? What is your name again? My name is Becky, she said. Becky, he repeated. Becky, can I kiss you? If you want to, she answered. My friend is waiting, he said. He pressed his mouth on hers waiting for her to open her mouth. He leaned back and said that was nice. Becky, you are a good kisser. He put the bottle down and settled next to her into the sofa. This is comfortable. He put his hand on her knee and started to stroke her leg. Is it okay if I do this? He looked at her closely. Yes, she said. What were you like when you were a little girl? Were you a daddy's girl? He picked up the bottle from the floor and took another swig from it. It is up to you whether my friend can come up. I think she is listening to the radio in the car. Is she young? Becky asked. Why, are you jealous? He looked at her watching him closely. No worries, Becky. You don't have to be jealous. A beautiful woman like you. Young like you, do you mean, or older and more experienced? He then guffawed. My friend is anything you want her to be. You don't have to be scared of me. I will not take advantage of you. My friend also has a body. Tell me about your wife, Becky said. She wanted answers. He didn't give her any. I need to straighten up a bit, Becky. Where is your bathroom? Straight ahead, she said. Be open to new experiences, she told herself. Be an open book. She didn't feel at all strange. She felt liberated. She was curious about the woman in the car. What did she look like? What was her childhood like? Was it anything like Becky's? Did she have an overprotective father as Becky had once had, who sheltered her from the world? A father who did not want her to go to the big city. Becky felt beautiful. The man was breathing down her neck now. Kissing her head. Running his hands up and down her back. Sit on my lap, Becky. She hesitated. Are you sure you don't want a drink?

Drink with me, Becky. Just have a sip. Becky took a sip and felt drowsy. The man guffawed. Yes, Becky, you are a bona fide woman now. She sat on his lap and leaned into him. Becky, I admire you a great deal, he whispered into her ear. This is what all girls must learn when they come to the bright lights of the big city. To be submissive. To be dominated. Are you sure my friend can't come up? I promise you we can have so much fun. We see with our eyes but we can also see through touch, say it is so, Becky. You are a woman now. What does that feel like? I feel different. The man guffawed loudly again. She can come up if she wants to. Your friend. She must be bored out of her mind by now, thinking that you have forgotten her. Becky took her shoes off. Standing up barefoot, in her slip, she made her way to the bedroom. Are you sure Becky? I don't want to corrupt you. I have the feeling you were raised in the church. I have the feeling you are a virtuous kind of girl. Raised with values and all of that. Does she have a name? Do prostitutes have names? Her name is Angel or Angela or something. She looks like an angel. You look like an angel too, except your name is Becky. She smiled when she heard him say her name. Do you smoke? Sometimes. Becky, what kind of answer is that? Either you smoke or you do not. When I feel stressed about something at work, that is the only time I smoke, Becky answered. Tell me about the hospital. Tell me about hospital life before I go and fetch my friend. I will read something I wrote about it to you, Becky said. I love it when people read to me. I am glad you feel different. He guffawed loudly again. Out of drinks. Are you sure you have nothing that I can wet my lips with in this place? Cute house though. You have made it very cosy. I like the arrangement of scatter cushions on your bed. It looks like you like to read many catalogues, to get ideas. Is that all you do with your spare time, Becky, read instead of living? I live for the moment. The man guffawed again. I don't think that I have ever met someone like you, Becky. I can't overlook how beautiful you look to me right now, the man said, stroking her head. Can I touch you, Becky, the way you have touched me, transformed me? Yes, you have transformed me into another man. Angela is waiting, Becky said. Sitting on the edge of the bed with her feet under her looking up at him. You are such an innocent child, Becky. I must corrupt you first. The man looked at her sadly. He took his tie off and then his jacket. You really don't mind if I corrupt you first, do you, Becky? You are a sharp one. You look at me like a girl but then again you also look at me like a woman possessed.

Are you a woman possessed, Becky? This is your cue, Becky. Either you will be corrupted or you will remain innocent. The choice is yours. I want you to corrupt me. I am tired of being innocent. All people see is what they want, projected onto their individual selves. They want to think that they are innocent when they are merely lost or at a loss for words. The man began to cry. I have children. I have a beautiful house. I have a wife. It doesn't matter to me anymore that I will never have those things, Becky said. I don't want any of it. They are beautiful things, they are not trophies. They keep me warm on cold nights, Becky. Books keep me warm on cold nights. Hot chocolate and literature. Abandon yourself, Becky said.

I carry these sorrows within my anatomy. My past overwhelms me sometimes with its urgency. Childhood is made up of mansions that have many rooms. There are extensions that are catalysts, sparks, and fireworks. The cracks in my childhood made up with their own alphabet. A neglectful mother who lacked insight into her own children's lives. A mother who never loved me. A father who was both father and mother. The culture that we live in as children exposes us to fragments of phenomenology. In the end, we are all scholars of trivia. We are all students of the school of life. Can you understand the property of dreaming? Silence between lovers who have known each other for a long time can be convenient sometimes. One person has their own thoughts. The other is lost in their own world. This lover lives in their own reality. That lover lives in their own reality. Each reality is stranger than fiction. Just as much as people can become estranged from their families, from their infirm and elderly parents, from their own arrogant, moneyed siblings, there is a wide-open space that is as vast as a desert. Life is always cosmic for visionaries. That is all they see. The awareness that others are not privy to. A woman lives in a cave. A man lives in his cave. The only time they ever meet is when they come out of their caves to look at the stars and to worship heaven. Humanity, human life, deals in that currency. They both realise that there is bleakness in this world. They both feel displaced when they leave the order and routine they experience in their cave. There is sadness in you. There is sadness in me. I project all fantasy onto you. You project the reflection of admiration onto me. We clothe ourselves in costume, in make-believe and in fancy dress. I wanted you to save me. You wanted me to save you in return. You have become significant to me in ways you cannot even begin to imagine. Talk to me about intimacy, he says, and I do my best but I talk like a girl and I walk like a girl. I wear my hair like a girl, piled on top of my head with bobby pins like I used to as a child when I went to ballet lessons in a church hall. Does he love me? Does he desire me? That is all I ever want to know from the men that I pass in the street, who sit in cafes drinking their coffee, eating their croissants. Men who are artists and men who are not artists. Men who were my English teachers. Men who were not my English teachers. Men who lectured me at college. Men I admired as I admired my own father. Men who are fathers and husbands. After all, they are the most important men. I know they will leave. I know they will betray me, in the end. They will teach me all they know of life. The contents and romanticism of their life experience. Their maladjusted behaviour, their rudeness, their tempers, their arrogance is what makes them who they are. The loveliness of their eyes, their anatomy, so different from mine, and their fine manners, their exquisite stories, which enthral me, make them who they are.

My father did not teach me these things. He only told me to be wary of them. The men that you work with. Do not ride with them in their cars to go to places with them. In the end, they will not respect you or love you. They will only condescend to you. Most of these types of men belong to an exclusive club called 'the elite'. They are wealthy. They love fast cars. They love smoking a certain brand of cigarettes and drinking whiskies in the evening. They love women. It does not matter even if they are married, they still love women. They are grown men who are still children. Children who still want to be worshipped and put on a pedestal. The men who belong to the elite are articulate, well educated. Some of them are intellectuals, and some are not. Be wary of them. They are sharks. There are shark-infested waters out there in the bright lights of the big city. You will find them everywhere. Around every corner. In every mall. In every family restaurant. They will look right through you. They will look you up and down. They will sweet-talk you. Whisper sweet nothings in your ear. They will give you gifts.

All of her bittersweet childhood Becky was brave, bold, brilliant. She felt she had to shout her existence into being from the rooftops of the city. Her tears were always diamond pinpricks. She always wanted to be saved, but from what she couldn't say, yet. She lost herself in music, in opera, the classical greats. She went to piano, swimming, speech and elocution, and drama lessons. She learned early on that there was an art to everything in life. There always had to be room for it in her life. She decided early on that her life always had to be governed by art. She always found herself picked last. She could not do handstands and cartwheels like the other girls. In high school, she didn't have a boyfriend. She had never been kissed. She was lonely. In the terrain of the city, she felt that all the life she was experiencing was putting space between her and her hometown. I am a woman now. She said it like a mantra. She soon faded into the squalour of the city.

It is my turn to talk now, said the man. Have you always been like this? Have you always written so beautifully? Have your eyes always been filled with so much self-doubt? I doubt if you have been this adventurous all your life. What would you like me to get you? No, I am being serious. I would like to get you something if it will make you happy. Daring to be someone else, not yourself. What is so wrong with you, Becky? Why the self-hate and the torture? Why self-sabotage? You manufacture touch. Venture through the sensory, understand the volition of the personality's intuition and you'll do it so well. With understanding, elegance and grace. Did your mother have elegance and grace? I see I have touched a nerve. Did the two of you not get along? Did your mother make many sacrifices for you? Did she ever touch you? Did she ever tell you how much she loved you? Why are you crying? Child. You are, after all, just a child, but I guess corruption took place long ago, before we even met.

Every man Becky had ever fallen in love with was beautiful to her. Their manners, their physicality, the impressions they left upon her marked her for life. She wanted them to possess her in exactly the same way that she possessed them. She wanted to master her traumatic childhood. She wanted to master the male and the female innerness of her soul. The spirit of the child that was still a part of her in adult life. She had an androgynous mind. She wanted to master pain and then when she realised her own sexuality she did master the pain that she had internalised for so long. Then it was finally released. It finally had an external world. Men were always something of a mystery. When they left her, of course she felt abandoned. When they didn't call her on the telephone, of course she felt neglected. She was an adult yet she still thought, acted and moved through the world like a child and with a child's intuition and velocity. She knew she had to explore the city. It had territories and districts filled with light and dark acts. This man just wanted to talk about her childhood.

Tell me about your childhood. Tell me about your mother. Do you look anything like her? Did she ever read your stories? I'm guessing not. I'm right. I'm always right. I shouldn't have spoken to you about my wife and children. There is always room for a young woman to grow and to learn from her mistakes. You will soon learn that a mistake is education in itself. Just don't end up loving me, regretting me or hating me for what I did to you. Sometimes men don't think when it comes to an inexperienced young woman. Men are creatures of empires and kingdoms. Women are creatures of habit. Women always want to fall in love. Yes, you do want that swimming pool and the kiddies. I know you do. I can see it in your eyes. I know what loneliness, isolation and rejection are. I have lived through all of that. It is only the beginning. The beginning of life. Nerves shaking. Anxiety-ridden, panic-stricken. It happens to the best of humanity. You should have banished me when you had the chance, then I wouldn't have exploited you. And yet you wanted to be exploited because you wanted to forget. You wanted to forget your childhood.

Perfume. The expensive kind. Becky finally told him what he wanted to hear and he smiled at her. A smile that was warm and genuine. Inviting her to smile with him as if they were playing a game. She knew she would recollect their conversations in a myriad of ways in her journal. One man became two, became three, became four, and became five and so on and so on.

When she telephoned her father every Sunday evening he would ask her, a slight tremor in his voice, when she was coming home. Did she have a boyfriend around her age yet? What kind of people had she met in the city? Certainly not the people you told me about, Daddy. Nobody is taking advantage of me. I am living my life. I am living my life on my terms. She was worried about what her father would say in return. Come home. Come home soon. You cannot live alone in the city like that. The city has shark teeth. Is there room for a cat or a goldfish? No, there was no room for a cat or a goldfish. What was that in the background, he would always say, anxiety rushing through him.

The man, it seemed, had a lot on his mind or he seemed to have momentarily lost his mind. He seemed to speak as if she was taking notes. As if she was his stenographer. You are useful in making me forget too. You want to regret something, regret me because that makes you forget the past. In other words, you can also say, I use you and you use me. We use each other. When you regret something, it is also a small triumph. If I kiss it better will it make it all right again? If I tell you that I love you, will you believe me? The sky is blue. You don't have to be. Tell me, what does it feel like to have lived your whole life near the ocean? Men want to believe that all girls are chaste. All girls want to be women. They want to get married and wear a wedding dress, wear flowers in their hair and that ring on their finger, but not you. You say it defiantly, as if you are taking a stand against something. For all the girls who have lost their way in this world. For all the girls whose mothers never loved them. For all the girls who are madly intellectual and surround themselves with literature.

Is there someone there with you, her father would say in a sing-song voice. It's nothing, Daddy, Becky would say. It's only the television. You can afford a television on your wages? Yes, I pay the TV off in monthly instalments. Let me go and switch it off. Do not get into the back seat of their cars. Oh, Dad, Becky would say biting her bottom lip. Becky, listen to me, come home. You will find someone nice, a decent man. You mean someone you approve of, Daddy? Oh, Becky. What has become of you? What is becoming of all your dreams, all your goals? Do you still feel inspired to write? There is a novel I am writing. But her father was not interested in that. Are you still a girl? Are you still my daughter? Daddy, please don't ask me that.

Daddy, I want to speak to Mum. Your mother is busy. She cannot come to the telephone right now. Oh, Becky. Why will you not give us your number? Where are you staying? Do you have a roommate or roommates? Please come home. The conversation would go back and forth like this. She could hear her mother in the background. What happened? What happened? You escaped. You found the exit. We all do, even men who are still boys at heart. You have a life. You have not failed at anything. You have dreams. You have goals. You inspire. You are creative. You have your little novel that you are writing and you are doing your best to cope, to act as if you have it all together, but anyone can see that not everything is all right in your world. Everyone can see that you are not coping. You are a late bloomer. Are you really living or do you live life like one of the protagonists in your stories? Do not say anything to me. You might regret it later. You have choices in life. I had to make choices too and at the end of the day, you are either a poor loser or the winner who takes it all. Do you know what your purpose is? Our purpose is to love and be loved in return. That should be the mantra of human life. This is what you have to do although it might sound very strange. You have to live. You have to give life a chance. If you do not, it is tickets for you. You will find yourself drowning in a pool of your own tears. Becky could hear her mother's voice. By now, she is probably a dancer in one of those clubs. That is what happens to girls like her. She is probably a dancer for money. Leave me out of the conversation. Becky could feel the diamond pinpricks of tears behind her eyes. Let go, let go, let go and surrender. She hates me. My own mother hates me, Becky thought to herself. Then I should go on living the way I do. I have a talent for it. For listening to shadows that wear masks and illusions that can strum guitar and violin strings illuminating truth and beauty. How do you know you are drowning even though you continually come up for air? It is not the truth that will set you free. People talk about emancipation all the time but do they actually know what freedom means? Here in the Johannesburg streets the air felt like no other. The people moved differently. Up streets. Down streets. Walking in alleys. There was always traffic everywhere she looked. All she wanted was silence. All she wanted was a room of her own. All she wanted was to write.

Self-pity is a terrible thing for a young woman to feel. It will turn you into a tragedy. I know what it feels like to have a young woman trembling in my arms. You are a girl. I know you want to be a woman but for now just be a girl. When you're older, you'll know what I'm talking about. Don't rush to get to a place where you will only feel older and more alone than you already are. I don't want that for you. (This man can talk like a woman, thought Becky to herself). You must have met many young men in your short life. No? Oh well, that is a surprise. Have you ever been happy? You have educated yourself well, I see from all the books around me. What do you want from life? Life is so short and the most precious thing about it is the love that human life and artists can express. If you are a writer, you are an artist. Your whole life is a ballad. Your whole life is made out of music. You are difficult. On the one hand, you want respect but with the kind of life you live now you will never find it. My name is Anita, said the girl when she finally came up the stairs. Why did you leave me waiting in the car so long? I thought you were never coming back for me. Oh, sorry. I thought it was Angelica. He stopped guffawing. This is your eternity, Anita said nastily. Tell her to stop looking at me like that. Do you understand what that word eternity means? Yes, Becky said. I do. This is my eternity, Becky repeated.

I am both Becky and Anita, dear Petya. I am also Gail. Who listens to smoke? Breath pumps through me. You're a symbol. You're good and kind folk. Perhaps you're a Lutheran now or Methodist. There's a story here. I find the supple words drowning in pathetic frustration, listless and lethargic yet alive. Bone is envious of flesh. Mother abandoned me. Father neglected Mother who in turn neglected me. I think back to those wasted years of my twenties and early thirties. I think of the rich men. I think of the rich men's character and personalities. How the rain always showered promises on top of my hungry head. I'm innocent. You're the devil. You're the devil walking around as if nothing can touch you. As if you're some kind of martyr. You're still living and breathing just like each of those rich men while I'm in need of prayer, reflection, introspection and meditation. Lucifer is my brother. My brother is the convict. Sexton was a beautiful woman. I'm an imposter. No woman am I. Plath was a brilliant poet. Please, please, don't ignore me. My tangled tongue carries winter news with it. I am mad somewhere in Africa. Pretty soon I guess it will evaporate. I'm running out of space. The words aren't there. I'm not safe to be around anymore. The sea just opened up. The sun has come for me. There's no us anymore. Why can't I just have one friend? Why do I have to be the one to watch my father die while my sister teaches English in Prague? I like this world now that you're in it. I'm old. I'm more aware of time slipping away. I am greedy for the gulls that fly overhead. The birds here fade into the sun. They worship there. Your face is sleeping. There's prophecy in the veins of driftwood. There's a prophecy in the birch, willow, walnut tree in the backyard. I'm in need of a cure for this sin I've been carrying. I'm abstract. I'm dressed to kill. There are flaws between these sheets that you need to be made aware of. My mother is a pretty woman. She was the prize. I'm a failure. I'm the failure in the family, her one failure. She is the vertigo above and below my mad dash into society.

I did not know my love had a wife. Daddy, Daddy, you're fading away. There's no place here for forgetting, only a place for the psychiatrist. Space seems to have taken up every conceivable realm and to even survive seems extraordinary. I'm like a rabbit or a fox down the hole. Smile, please smile, I say to my reflection in the bathroom mirror. I wish to drown, fall, escape, drown, fall, escape, drown and find the key. Find the way out. Again, there's isolation. Sleep deprivation. Again, I'm counting sheep. I know I have a history of it. Again, again, again, this vision that you have is big. All the paternal relatives printed this invisible writing on my chest. Once she was the light of my life. Now all I know is that this world is an inhumane place. She knows what is wrong with the company she keeps. I keep finding gurus. The girls here are models. Please tell the rest of the case-studies, all the psychologists, I'm learning how to forgive and forget. I'm learning to surrender. Please, look at my aunt, isn't she kind? She cooks and she cleans and she carries my dreams wherever she goes. She brings with her the glory of the flock of my maternal family. She gives my madness the courage to grow. Please tell someone, anyone who cares to listen, who has the willpower to open their heart wide open; the family doesn't think this behaviour is cute anymore. That the world is a space made up of dark matter. It becomes a circle that swallows me whole blue wrists and all. I don't have a swarm inside of me growing arms and legs. I don't have it in me to bring progeny into the world.

Children play in the river of mercy, grace and dust and dirt. They play at making mud pies, drinking tea, wearing their mother's high-heeled shoes. Their minds are unquiet although they are seen, visible to the adults around them. The tormented unquiet is often silent but the wound is there. There were times when my siblings and I felt abandoned by our parents. They had so much happening in their own lives. Grown up stuff that we didn't know how to deal with yet. We were all thirsting for the love of the perfect adult human, mother or father. Our life as a family was flawed, but also magnificent. It was never boring. We knew we were different because of our dad. He was our strength. He was the master of our universe. A kind of Archie. A kind of comic book hero who could do no wrong although he was both clumsy and cute at the same time. It was hilarious and fabulous at the same time. It was surreal, beside the sophisticated high art that was my mother, that beautiful, otherworldly, elegant dream of a woman. Fathers are special people. You tell them your list of goals and they inspire you to reach them. They are the ones standing on the side-lines, mouthing the words 'I love you' and 'I think that you are brilliant' when you feel that you weren't as brilliant as you should have been. They are the first ones you go to when you feel sad or when you are happy. All my life that is what my father did. He wasn't all of those things all of the time. Sometimes he was sad, and as a child it made me feel angry and confused when he cried or was upset. Now, I imagine him as a young adult, as a hunter. A lonely warrior whose brain was bursting out of his skull, his brain cells tormented by the Periodic Table, smashed up against elegant words like bilateral symmetry, biology, anatomy, dissection, zoology and mitochondria, surrounded by mountains of books, hills and green valleys of physics and chemistry textbooks. He wanted to become a medical doctor but life had other plans, and he became a teacher and a writer. He has been writing all his life, and even now he is always in pursuit of something. His soul is like that constellation beyond the trees, like a dreamcatcher. Ancestral, universal. I do think that I am a poet because of him, my beautiful shadow that always lingered in my presence. As the void of his depression coloured his world, so it coloured mine. Depression can be seductive, like a ballad of winter trees, of nature imagined into being, a transition to a startling leap of faith when your spirit is awakened to the highest of humanity. But seeing the world through those blurred lines isn't pretty. It comes with its own addictions, though it didn't drive my father to drink or to the violence I saw in other families. My father is my best friend. I have talked to him in the early hours of the morning about anything and everything. He has inspired me, given me hope and energy, helped me to make up with my mother and my sister. He challenged me to think a great deal about literature, science and history, complex, out of the box subjects. He poured wisdom with a divine ceremony into his three children's minds. He was a catalyst, and to me he was a kind of god in his principal's suit, reading the newspaper while I obediently finished my ice cream. His life story reads like a book of secrets, claustrophobia, vertigo and therapy and it has set my life on a trajectory that is out of my hands. He is frailer now. He is in the autumn of his years. Sometimes he forgets things. Sometimes he is stubborn as hell. Sometimes he is arrogant. Sometimes he is as petulant as a child. He is the fragile one now. He is the one that needs to be taken care of. Once upon a time, he was the caretaker, the breadwinner, the nurturer and now I have to pay it back. I remember the day after Boxing Day. I heard my parents talking, the television in the background, my mother quiet for once, relaxed. My father was eating meat prepared on Christmas Day, what was left of the gammon, roast chicken and beef with creamy potato salad, beet stains on his T-shirt, his feet bare, and his belly hanging over his swim shorts. They were both watching the cricket. He scratched himself on his legs. They were in love once. They shared a first kiss, held hands, held onto each other in the dark at the drive-in, dated, wooed each other, and wrote love letters. My father sent postcards from the continent as he travelled through Europe on holiday from his studies at London University. Now he washes the dishes, cleans his bathroom, sweeps out his bedroom. He mops and dries the tiles. It upsets me, somehow, to see him like this. I look at my father now with love, respect and in awe. All I want to do is honour him, and his memory.

Did I tell you, Mother, that I love your third eye? And did I tell you I'm crazy for your love, for you? I'm a bad feminist hungry for you. Don't forget all about me. If you do, I'll haunt you for the rest of your life. Even the paintings in our house speak a language. There's an accident-prone child in the house. You don't belong to me anymore, anymore. And the sane tigers come at night. You're a hunter. You're a photograph. You're a story. For my flesh and blood sisters I've fixed my anxiety with sorcery. Let it all out. I let it all out. She was the most beautiful thing I had ever seen. They'll say one day, While she had stars in her eyes, night and day bathed in her flesh. I followed the law's world. I carried a knot of tenderness in my heart for her heart, my cracked soul for hers; my spirit lived for her spirit. The game of being estranged from my complicated family is what I'm good at. How do I deal with that criminal rejection? You have given me your church. Spread your message of love to the world. All I ask is that you believe in me, as I have believed in wise, wise you, good feminist. I keep on finding nuns where I should be finding you. You're Atlantis. You're a rhyming avalanche, my beauty. You're beloved by men. You're on fire for their adoration. You're a know-it-all going through life with a permanent smile on your face. But me, I'm afraid I'm going down that cold road that leads to nowhere fast. It's as hot as hell out there today. You'll find waves of desire in sanity. You'll want to call a 'normal' reality, a strange new world, home. We can be blind to our own faults, our own flaws, and I remember when we didn't have much in the way of anything. We had each other and that was enough. You were noble and I was a prince. This year I fixed up the garden of anxiety and death for you. I still remember how I stunned you when I called your heart home, and sanctuary.

Here is my alter ego, Gail. Things of the past, things of the future. There are so many things going through Gail's head. The sea, part natural, part supernatural, spits driftwood out, a log, so much life, so much life, so much life. The river runs to it, asking for the taking. Gail falls, blue, she sleeps the sleep of the dead. The dead do not struggle against all the odds, on their terms to live, they sanction the most beautiful part of their lives. What is not celebrated in life is celebrated in death, and in the water. Gail is like a fish. Her father is not a tall man. He's a cheating man with women on the side, a man's man, he is fading away into autumn, branches are growing out of him, his fingers are an offering to God, sucking up all the clay, and the rain. All Gail wants to do is drain the paradise of the morning, she thinks she's in love, but he's older than she is. Her father does not smoke anymore. There's a sadness to the day. Gail swims laps bravely. In her thirties, she swims laps bravely, and when she gets out of the pool, her father towel-dries her hair. The smell of the rain covers her like a wedding veil, and the earth is like a shroud. Gail takes a warm bath when she gets home. Her father reads one of her fashion magazines looking at the women in lingerie, and bikini tops, and bottoms. She removes all the articles of clothing that she is wearing, lights up a cigarette, sits on the edge of the bath, and smokes her heart out. She puts her hand in to test the water. Lukewarm. Just right. She slips into the water, mapping her feet out, watching her pink toes. She has forgotten to put the bath oil in, and the Epsom salts for her sore muscles. She reads poetry in the bath. New Inscapes. She reads about Alan Paton's reformatory boy, and cries, and cries. Her breasts are too small, she sometimes feels she's too short, and all she wants to do is marry this older man, but he already has a wife, and a daughter, and a high-profile career. She thinks she can be a devoted mistress. Quiet, and unseen. Fit to be lover, physical body, dolphin belly, her psyche belonging to the married man, only to him. Gail is pink from her bath. The sexual impulse is far removed from her. All she wants is the older man to take her into his arms. To have a child with him. For him to make love to her, to go for long walks with her by the sea, her sea, the sea of her childhood. The sea inspires madness in her, something vast, something remote, something complicated like loneliness, and fear and anxiety. Gail feels the fear most days. She can't get away from it. She paints her toenails red, listens to rock music blaring from her radio, makes her hair fluffy. She wonders if in the eyes of her older man she is sexy. If she is a Lolita. She wonders about the gestures Betty Blue makes in that French film, and wonders at her sadness. For it seems to Gail that all French women, although they are truly beautiful, are also sad creatures always meeting up with men, giving themselves body, soul, and spirit to them, and then, then the men just let them go. Gail is reading Mikateko Mbambo's poems now. A girl who goes to Pretoria University. She's not from Zimbabwe, as Gail first thought, nor from South Africa, but this is neither here nor there for Gail. The poems leave her breathless. The poems are like evening blossoms, blossoms of women in the daylight. Gail goes quiet. The curry burns at the bottom of the pot. She is supposed to watch the curry, so that it doesn't burn at the bottom of the pot. The poems are like the gathering of elders, the matriarchs and patriarchs of a village, and they've all come for a feast. The sangoma is also there to bless the feast. In Mikateko's poetry there's a kind of undergrowth, of memory, that exists in the children playing at the feast, becoming conscious of the adults' world, the kissing games of the older kids, and the adults see the future, as Gail sees her future, and the future of these poems travelling across the world like sunlight, and nerves. They're like amoeba-slime in the adrenaline of a male world. And years pass by Gail in minutes, and she thinks of the solitary figure of the female sangoma at this feast, and there's blessing too. Blessing in these poems. Afterwards, she washes her hair in the kitchen sink, shaves her legs. It feels as if she is getting her period. The poems are filled with longing, and belonging, the glory days of her youth, of, no doubt, Mikateko's youth too. Gail feels very much innocent. Gail thinks that all poets have lived, and loved. Gail thinks she hasn't lived at all. In her bedroom, she's like a typhoon. In the mornings she wakes up, feels ugly because her older man, whom her father knows about, hasn't called her. It feels as if he's forgotten all about her.

She checks her emails, but there's no message from him, and it feels as if she's on her way out of his life for good. She has poetry in her life, to save her from falling, and the poems are like a gun going off. The wind sighs outside; mid-afternoon, Gail puts on a jersey. Her mother is a florist, and works all day until her fingers are numb to the bone, and she feels like death on her feet. She comes home after five, braving peak traffic in her family sedan. It is cold, getting colder still, the sun disappears into the sky, becoming a thing of the past, and a thing of the future. Gail makes tea, takes her ginkgo biloba, and feeds the tomcats. Inside, after that swim, her stomach muscles feel like a drum. She scrubs the sweet potatoes under the tap in the kitchen sink, until the water runs beautifully clear. Put them in the oven, because that is the way her mother has eaten them ever since she was a little girl on the farm in Ladysmith. The earth is black after the rain. The sea is green after the rain, Gail remembers that. The sea is like the sun, old. Gail is quiet and slow in the afternoon. She's tired. The bath in the middle of the day has made her tired, but at the root of it all, she is a hungry reader. She thinks she'll find the way home in her lover's arms, but she knows she won't. She jumps a little too far, swears her love to him, sees starlight and wonders in his eyes, but that's all there is. That's all that she sees. She swears to her father that her lover is attentive, and romantic, but it's a half-truth. She feels low. The only thing that she trusts these days is the poetry, Bessie Head's *Maru*, and Athol Fugard slipping into word-kill. Her heartbeat pulsates every time she reads *The Road to Mecca*, and she thinks of how handsome Gavin Hood was on the stage when he won the Oscar for Best Foreign Language Film. She dreams about Johannesburg, her winters there, her aunt's house freezing even though they lit a fire in the fireplace. They'd roast marshmallows. Gail remembers her cousins. Too beautiful, too desirable for their own good. They married young, in their twenties. They had their babies in their twenties. Gail had never been engaged, never had a serious boyfriend, never received a wedding, or engagement, or promise ring. In the water, she was a platypus. The poems were like brushstrokes to her, opened her up to vulnerability, and intimacy, and the shame of apartheid. The dreams young men had in those days, and the girls who wanted to become women, and the wives who were deeply unloved, had men for husbands who sought female partners, not just a wife to be kept at home to cook and clean, barefoot and pregnant, mopping the kitchen floor.

Gail didn't really understand apartheid, didn't remember it. What was wrong with interracial relationships anyway? Gail felt that she had to apologise for it, as if apartheid had been all her fault. Zuma spoke of social cohesion. But what did that mean, anyway, to black people, who were the majority stakeholders in South Africa? It stung her. Apartheid shamed her. But she knew that life for black people was filled with shocking despair, trauma after trauma incident, hardship. The pain they felt was like a fire in their belly. They had been forced to speak English, to learn English like machines, women working on an assembly line, and all she could see was their post-apartheid sense of inferiority, and the superiority complex of her earth, and sky, and sea.

Mother, a stranger and a friend. But the air is growing cold. As cold as the angst of beginners. I am not that scholarship girl in chapters and parts. I keep on forgetting to ask her how she is. She keeps on forgetting to tell me. There's a paradigm shift from her. From the seat of her lava smile to her oracle-textured and mother-in-law laughter, clothed in virgin garments, her hands anointed with coconut oil. She's never said she's fought for me. The architecture of her bones stays in my mind. Life with daughters, life with son, life with grandchild mocks me. This vanishing tribe of family has left me to see the existential world. The glass is half-empty. All I can see is this downpour of grieving in my heart. She wants to take everything.

She already has everything. But the light saves me at the end of the day. I'm tired of this loneliness. It is my heart that is supernatural-uttered. I want her to remove all her sin from me. The sin, the sin, it lingers like vertigo. Her lack of love speaks to me of romps in decay, a wild dagga swamp where the sunlight was a harsh mad-cold. It had no maps. No roads. Only stability in a facility that had no coastal views. Offered us no freedom. Once I lived in a different world. I was free then. She was the ghost and I was the darkness that she dared not speak of. She, the divine feminine. This bone bouquet. This flesh, this lovely olive skin, but I'm ashamed. You see, I've always been taught to be ashamed of the colour of my skin. Freedom breaks, just like a wave, just like a branch, breaks away from the trough meeting peak, and I dream of my mother-tongue fastening itself upon your mother-tongue. You are a muse, you know I'm coming up for air. I think of the high care ward at the posh clinic I was at. How I overcame it. African blood is powerful. That's why I write the way I do. Ankles deep in water. The sea exists to flow for another thousand years. Its purity lit up at night. Jenny Zhang, Dorothea Lasky, give me back the illusion of the modern-day glamour of the contemporary female poet.

The sinful phoenix in my life, my brother, wants to get away to Canada like a thief that comes in the night. Brother, you look as if you taste prayers, mantras, your sad guitar playing an altruistic gospel affair. Brother's soul was as brief as the ocean and he followed this, the decay of his flaming lips. Read this ignorant joy found on blue hills, the love story of the sea's forsaken rapture and vision. I've known circles of pain to poison. Who you love can make you feel beautiful from the inside out. Your tiny bones like the stimulus and vigour of waves. Your smile promises me speech. Brother, Nietzsche. I think of his catatonic state towards the end of his life. Of how when Dad went to church in his wheelchair my brother was nowhere to be seen or found. That was his act. To destroy the river in my father's eyes. I don't like how he speaks to me. When he speaks to me, I wish I was dead. I wish that you could understand me. I'm frightened of living now. I am a fossil adrift; the shimmer of flesh and I go bone-crazy, doomed valleys. You're like chameleon music in the valleys of my inner world, my sanctum. You're hoping. Little earthquakes inside their heart. Glass bastards, every one. They eat her alive until they're sated. Animals. Carnivores feasting. They give burning driftwood a name. The beasts. The kiss of death on her lips. Once again, the violence of child rape in the morning newspaper, or on the evening news. The end game, ice and glass in their eyes. It is a mad, dark sea. Hyperactive boys. Pain, brutally articulate. Electric pangs of hurt are the price every poet must pay. Indentation of men on her otherness, body. Flames of violent emotion. Flood of loneliness. Obsession with vice, and the surgical instruments to put her fleshy parts back together again. Light me up. Light every woman, child, boy or girl up. They have done something bad. Something evil. Currents of evil flash through the air. All ten fingers and all ten toes glimpse at what is not natural. Nocturnal devils' devilish desires. Echoes of poison, hysteria's grace. They want her to beg for her life. The drugs make her high. Intoxicated. She's dead inside. Her soul withers into a numb cold, indifferent country. They make her think it is all in her fragile head, that she was the one who made them do it. Out of the black comes a crying in the rain. Little earthquakes like spokes on a wheel. The sea flows lava, flows and flows, and the sea is favour, the river is grace and forms of radiance. I invest leaves into the mimic-cry-wolf of winter news that appears with the snow. I'm falling into the arms of rain. Look! The traveller has arrived. He hides the weak force of his nose in the river. The snow storm, the winter nights whirl cloud-like supported by the fresh and new threshold of the self-portrait of the reflection of Diana Ferrus, the South African poet. I watch the news. Child rape on the news again. Tragedy breaking me into a million burdens. In each house there's either a rape or a tragedy. I choose to go to the sea. I choose to burn up and adjust the heat of the sun. I choose to live there. Drinking in the refuge of a tornado, the summer tunnels made out of paper beckon. I believe in you. That you're a custom-made reckoning made from the woodland-rib of Adam. You're no longer sin. You no longer have a sinful nature. Take this liberty. Take this. Lines composed of nature, composed of the natural.

I wrote sonnets for you. You puckered up your lips and kissed me. Calling me your Zelda. Your Clarissa. I gaze upon your possessions. Kneel to receive you. Give your body all the praise and worship. Seeing is a wasted life. Pull me through. It felt like a marriage. The smell of sex in the bedroom. Been that way now for over twenty years and still he didn't want to commit. Still my love, my heart, my soul wasn't enough. And he left. He left for Cape Town to lecture at the university. Met someone. An actress in the drama department. Younger than me. Older by a few years, more mature than me. More confident in her desire for him. He couldn't wait around. He made me cry in his arms and he would hold me tight in his warm embrace and then he would let me go and go home to his family. Buy me dinner in a fancy restaurant, and afterwards we'd have sex and he'd whisper my love, my love, my love, in my ear. When we went to hotels, we'd pretend to be the Roosevelts (I'd be Eleanor and he'd be Theodore), or Scott and Zelda Fitzgerald. Of course, I knew it couldn't last forever. My moods went up and down. Even when I was on my period. He hated coming over then and I knew in my heart of hearts it wouldn't last forever. Simpatico. And the separation was always so difficult to deal with. But when we were together it was like fireworks. I was a virgin. Virgin territory he called me, every time, every single time when he went down on me. I would climax immediately, and sometimes he'd smoke a cigarette before and sometimes he'd smoke a cigarette after. Sometimes, he'd roll a joint, I'd say that it gave me a headache, and this would make him smile. I have a long memory for painful things. Let's dance. And sometimes when he wanted to do something new in bed, well, I was inexperienced and just wanted to please him. I just wanted to make him happy. He was my boyfriend and I loved and respected him and looked up to him. I mean, he was my entire life. My entire life was work, work, work, study, study, study, and then when I met him, I just fell in love. And for him, I discovered later, it was just sex, sex, sex. He wasn't looking for a mother substitute. It was me. The whole time it was me. I was looking for a father substitute. Yeah, for sure, he told me that he loved me. He told me that he cared about me. Would love me forever and forever. And I would be his muse and inspiration. Did I tell you? I'm going to America. I'm leaving the memory of the love of my life, and all of this. The stuff between my dad and my mother behind me. I feel like an Avenger. I feel like Captain Marvel. I'm leaving on a jet plane, and as I speak, Steven Tyler of Aerosmith is whisking me away to Armageddon, although I'm not perfectly happy about it because I wanted him to come with me, you see, you see. I wanted him all to myself. But when I call now, she answers the phone. When she hears my voice, she hangs up. In the past she, his wife, the mother of his three children, used to tell me not to phone, not to waste my time. That she knew I had so much potential. So much to give. So much love inside of me. Now she tells me to leave them alone. He has a wife. He makes love to her. She, his wife and the mother of his three children tells me that I should get a job. Perhaps I should move to another country. Teach English there. I mean, I mean, I could do that here. I could teach English in a rural area, live in the countryside. Still see him on the side. Still love him, and we'd be inseparable together. You see, I keep telling myself that. He was the first man who told me that I was sexy and looked cute in jeans, a boyfriend t-shirt, and my scuffed leather boots. He told me that he loved me with nothing on. He told me that he loved me in bed. That this was more than just a romance, or an affair to remember. It was a scenario. Landscape. He used that kind of language with me. He said when he was with me, when we were still together, still a couple, he was living vicariously through me, the life he'd had when he was a student at the Vancouver film school. Whenever he could break away from his domestic disturbance. Not, note, domestic goddess. He called her a domestic disturbance, and the children, three spoiled brats. Talented brats, inventive brats, curious brats that drove him crazy with love. I drove him wild in bed, he said. I gave him his youth and vigour and vitality back. I was the perfect girl for him and once he even said I reminded him of his wife. My thighs, my legs, my well-toned arms, the way I wore my hair in bed turned him on. He called it 'bed hair'. Messy and unkempt hair, preferably wearing nothing. He'd make me climax again and again and again. He told me once, he and his friends took a road trip to Utah. To the Sundance Film Festival. He thought he caught a glimpse of Casey Affleck and once he thought he saw Robert Redford actually coming out of a coffee shop. Yes, yes, yes. I was in love with him. I'll be in love with him for the rest of my life. Pieces of me intertwined with his wife, his children, the children that I could never have. I love him. I still love him. I feel old. Inside I feel the terror of missing out on so many things. I gave him the best years of my life. They've just renewed their vows, bought a mansion in Constantia. She's a writer too. She writes screenplays. I write books. I see them all the time, in the gossip columns in the tabloid newspapers, or she's on the cover of a local fashion magazine. I believe in going for walks, I believe in parks and trees. They talk about their work or their family life. That could have been me, I tell myself when I'm really, really high. Tell myself that that is just my superego talking, talking about absolutely nothing, and that I know in reality would never be true. Together, as husband and wife, we would have fought all the time. He would have felt misunderstood. I would have felt like the third wheel in the relationship with his children, and believe me, they are not much younger, or older, than I am. I think to myself, what have I lost, what have I gained. A book. A gorgeous novel. Some poems that have even won awards. I've graduated with honours. Summa Cum Laude, but then again, none of that really matters to me anymore. It didn't matter to him. It didn't make him want me. It didn't make him want to love me. I don't really have family. I lost touch with my mother and sisters over the years. Never went to weddings. Can't stand them. Never went to my dad's funeral. Never really understood the personal velocity of having a relationship with a man who was old enough to be my father. I think to myself now, what a wonderful world it was when he was in it. I felt so sophisticated all the time. Now I just feel down. I just feel low. His wife is beautiful. They all look perfect together. I made the right decision in the end, didn't I? To leave him be. Not to fight for him. It wasn't love actually. Fire of my loins, light of my life, a place called home. How the heart behaves. He called it nice. He would say, call it generalising, that the relationship we had was nice, and gentle, and easy, and once he even used the word persuasive. He called it fun. And I think for most men going through a midlife crisis, sex with someone much younger than they are is just a distraction until their wife gives birth, or returns home alone from a work function, or returns from a conference in Pretoria, or a film festival in Burkina

Faso where she's on a panel discussion. Now I go for younger men. Pretend I make up the rules as I go along.

Everywhere I go, I'm alone. I eat breakfast alone. I eat my lunch alone. I eat my microwave suppers alone. I'm on a bus and I'm alone. I buy flowers. Read J.D. Salinger. I'm in this beautiful park, just looking at the landscape and the trees. They're birches, I think. I look at the people passing by, babies in their strollers, and I'm completely, completely, utterly alone. I miss him. I miss the two of us together. Simpatico. I'm alone. He has his family. I turn 70 next year. He turns 90. I'm supposed to be happy. But I'm not. I should have fought for him then, but I didn't. All I have is books, books and more books. Fifty books in total. Awards are nice. But I share them with an empty apartment. Wealth and privilege, status and power, drive and a certain kind of ambition in women mean nothing to me at all. I'm staring at the kitchen cupboards again. Slinking around the house in my robe. He gave me hope. Petya, I'd rather have him, now, here, with me, in Australia, than have it all. He killed all the love I had inside of me. I don't know how to love me anymore, or anyone else for that matter. I haven't spoken to him in years. Years and years. All I remember is being too young. Too young, stupidly in love, you see. Alone in this park, this afternoon. I want to feel him against me again. See him laugh. See him smile. Tonight, I'll feed my cats. Go to bed early, or write, or watch rubbish television. Try and forget that love is just part of the game of life. I just, I just can't seem to move on. I'm in God's hands now, eating chicken soup for Africa, collecting empty boxes. I want to forget. Boys, men, father substitutes. Place them in a box. Boots and all. Everybody has to grow up sometime.

Today is going to be the day that I am going to fall in love with you. To me you're like the vision of Einstein, John Legend, DMX, Eminem all rolled into one. I sing, and I find I'm singing to you. I dance, and I feel like you're watching me from afar. When I wake up, I look into the mirror, I see you. My days are kept waiting for you. My nights are kept waiting for you. I'm waiting for your face like an assignment. It's hard to believe what you've done for me, and to me. You are a hurricane in my heart. I think of you all the time. Sleep at night, only to wake and think of you. Holding you, kissing you, touching you. All of this. Haven't thought about sex in years. Haven't thought about making love, in years. You need me. I need you. The world was an insanely ugly wreck before. Now it is infinite. Static in my head. A river in my tears. My soul is on fire for you. All I do is wait for you. Change my clothes. Dream up that I'm beautiful for you. Do you think I'm beautiful? Do you find my personality as attractive as I do yours? People look at me, and they laugh. I think you know this about me already. I'm trying to move on. Trying to think that I love you. Only you. But we've both been here before. In bed, with other people, other women for you. I mean what I say. Now all I see are your brown eyes. It's just sex, my love. Messing around. We're both adults now. Grown-ish. We can do what we like, so long as it's not hurting anyone. So long as we know that there are two people involved, you, and me. And it will be our secret. Take off your clothes, or would you prefer that I do that for you? I'll go down on you. Down low. I'll go deep, I promise. You're the most beautiful thing that I've ever seen in my life. *C'est la vie.* Life goes on. Will we make it? You like the kind of girls you like. I like grown men who are unavailable and attached to the hip of their wives and children. Truth. You'll mess me around. I'll mess with your mind. I don't think that you'll mind all that much. You've been in love before. Even have the wedding ring to prove it. Nobody has loved me in this wilderness. I wish

I could be beautiful for you in ways that only you can imagine. I need stability in my life. You need stability in your life. Already, I know that I'm not your type. It's just fun.

A woman who has been abused doesn't know how to trust. She either hates men, or becomes promiscuous. She realises that she wants love, and that she needs love and that that love is only forthcoming from Jesus Christ. She usually prays the same prayer at night. Help me. Please help me. God are you out there? Jesus Christ, are you listening to me? Nobody loves me. I am ugly, selfish, worthless and pathetic. Today I only ate a yoghurt, a carrot stick and a lettuce leaf. She tries her hardest to understand why she is always walking away from relationships. Why did her mother take her innocence as a small child? She blames herself for what happened. She only knows how to abuse other people and doesn't understand what unconditional love is. She keeps waiting for someone to show up. She keeps waiting for someone to save her. She doesn't understand that only Jesus Christ can save her.

Is it too late, she asks herself, for the man of her dreams, for Robert was always the man in her dreams, to save her again? Does she perhaps have a future with him, at his side? Will he ever understand why she walked away from the warmth in his arms? Why did she walk away from Johannesburg, why did she walk away from the husband that she had been looking for her entire life? God, she says, if he still wants me, is still unmarried, or if he is married, bless him, bless Pamela, bless the people that he works with, who love him. In spite of twenty years, in spite of the age difference, his vast life experience, her limited life experience, she wants to know if he would still love her. I want to know if he would still love me, Petya. Perhaps you and I are like the zebra and the giraffe. The wisest ones. I'm looking for the star sign of a fortunate man in the realms.

I won't fly into you again. You won't come around like clockwork on a Sunday evening. I'm a flame in a pantomime. Look out for the sleeping satellite. You're gone into the arms of another woman. You're velvet, but taste like regret. Guess this is just a veil. I've romanced you. You've seduced me. I'm learning that I'm a celestial. You're free. Goodbye mysterious lover. Goodbye never boyfriend. Again, I'm dying inside. I look within. I say goodbye with my head held high. Guess I won't be invited to the wedding, or the wedding reception. Too much history there. Here. In the dark. Goodbye, old friend. Didn't know we could have spent eternity together. So much wasted potential. I'll always understand you. You me. So much wasted time.

I let the years go by. You were loved. Take that with you. You were a cherished friend once. Now you're in love. Don't return my phone calls. You're free. I understand everything now. Look at me. Let go. I'm already gone. Faded into memory. Don't speak. Don't speak. You do that so well. I will always love you. That is all I am taking with me. She'll be your wife, and it cuts like a knife. I had feelings for you once. I've surrendered you to the universe. It gave you a wife. Your wife is your hope now. Your hands. I'm no superwoman. Don't even have a man to call my own. No one like the one I love. I've gone the distance. Followed my heart. Tell you something. Must be karma. Read the books your father read, people say. I waste time. I waste time. I read books. Sometimes when I do, I cry. I don't need a shield for the emotion. I'm letting go. I'm saying goodbye. You're still beautiful to me.

This morning the love of my life said that she didn't care for me, to listen to me. Perhaps sisters are like that. I don't love the men anymore. They've gone to the cemetery of the mind. I'm not ashamed of anything I've done. I don't have any regrets. I never started a war. Once I was under his spell, but he never chose me. I read books. He wanted to hide me away from the world. I remember his sad songs. They kill me now. I tried to fall in love, I failed, but I'm wiser now. I tried to teach him that I was hurt too, Petya, but he walked right on by, said goodbye. I wanted to say, please don't go, but he didn't give me a chance. He just made me wise. Don't dedicate anything to me, he said. I'm not that kind of person. Did Einstein have fangs like me, did he love like me? For sure, science stopped his heart. You were always there, Petya. I'm blue. I've been wounded, eyes on fire with no cash. Time has all the answers, whether you want to decode the moon, the planets, the sun, or just want to love, fall in love, leave a lover. My lungs are made of iron, and flightless bird. I want everything that my heart wants. Whom will I love eventually? Who will love me for a lifetime, an eternity? I'm tired of waiting. It feels like I've been waiting forever. There are micro cuts on my fake heart. He's gone. I am done leaving my sorrows behind. And all I want to be is with the older men with their premium brands of cigarettes. Take me up there all the time. Take me. Take me to the museum. Teach me to love him. Teach me to care for him. To bury my secrets deep. I'm falling like a flightless bird. A flightless little bird, scared, yet still flying. And I still believe in freedom, you know that.

Petya, you're king. Your land is king. Your ocean-sea is king. Together we go. I'm going to make a mistake. I'm going to get gone. No one loves me in this place. Waiting for someone to save me is useless. It kills me to say that nobody loves like I do. That I matter like nuclear energy, to no one. I'm fucking priceless. No one's around. So I walk alone. Always on my own. No more hurt now. Only triumph. No more trials. Step back, wolf. Don't embrace me. I'm a ghost in the wilderness. Ghosts don't change anyone. Just an illusion shaped like a human being. The river of dark nights. I'm dead to the world. It came from Japan. It came from Hiroshima's loneliness. This rain that is falling is a miracle. No one wants that person's reflection in the mirror. Nobody misses her. She remembers all of their wounds, her wounds, his wounds. She's torn by the miracle now. What does it matter that I wish I was dead? Let go of me. Drunk on seawater and tragedy. Hate me. Petya, would you rather be a man, or a woman of genius? I am a poet half-formed by the sea.

I am a woman now, growing older and I must learn to endure everything. Beneath my skin, my heart beats faster and faster. I have often wondered what the diagnosis is. Perhaps it is a fear of being found out that I am so desperate to be loved. The confusion of my childhood played itself out with the older sky above me. Hell, down below me, where I was a guest, treated me like royalty. The cat was warm, inspiring me to sleep this afternoon. Sleeping in the middle of the day is a sure sign of depression. I covered my body with the sheet and blankets, rested my head on the cool spot on the pillow but I could only see a dark forest that smelled of dew when I closed my eyes and an outline of a woman who wore a red coat in the moonlight. I couldn't make out her features, this witch; was she a ghost with her hands covered in blood? Was she Lady Macbeth spiced up, in disguise? An accomplice to something much more sinister, her own death? And why was she bleeding? I pulled the covers over my head like a veil. You are dreaming, I told myself. I could have screamed. Instead, I kissed her on her cold mouth to comfort the poor thing. She seemed so unfulfilled, as lost as I felt. I didn't want her to leave me. She kept me company, gave me the feeling of making me want to live. So now, the question: 'Is what I describe a hallucination or am I just talking crazy?' When you are crazy, you do not know that you are electric. I have visions. I am okay with that. I know that it scares people. Honesty scares people. I am okay with that too. There are days that I take my pills and dress and then I wait. I wait for the laughter or the panic or the anxiety, whichever comes first, to show up and make waves. Some days I am okay and then I know it's going to be a good day, all good, more, now, again. I am one of the lucky ones.

You're a prophet, Petya. You're a compass. Your reflection is a compass. The picture of winter. The picture of a winter leaf. And in the face of a river there are spaces that are ungovernable and spaces that need to be governed in the shadow of the afternoon sun. On water and on land my youth is finished. I am dying to belong. People will try to capture in words and pictures what the drought and famine of love really means. I have never been in love properly. There is the flesh in my hands. There is the flesh in the room, a prize like the milk of electric love. There is the flesh in the mirror. It hurts. Love hurts. I am a woman. I am a woman in the dead of night. A winter night. The streets are deserted. When I was younger, I was scared of growing up. Now I am afraid of growing older. Of being eternally bloom-less. It is a real winter's day in summer. The gust of wind is picking up little by little, spreading itself around. I must clean out the fridge with a soft cloth and vinegar. My other self. I remember when I was young, and all I had was inexperience. Now I am older, and all I have is experience.

The continent constructs us and not the other way around. It folds and blinds us under its wings. It has saved my life. I have been at the worst of times needy, clingy and self-absorbed even with the best of intentions. It drives me mad, to forget, blankets us under the moon, stars and sun and faith. God melts our hearts; or is it the eyes? With every pulse, every fluttering heartbeat it smells of brutal rage as much as it does imagination. We fall under the spell of its geography, the bones of its half-fall. The silver linings of its humanity. The human condition, its tragedy, is staged. Are poets sly? I am only awakening now as a poet. I feel this emptiness, this cold inside of me sometimes. Tricky in my head. Always in my head. I think of the poets who hide the whiskey at the bottom of the drawer in their desk. Does this mean dishonesty, that all is not well? Then I think of the burning world of Eve, daughter of Eve, son of Adam. I think of the smile lines on my face. I think of sad laughter. Do all poets feel this way, want to feel this way? I try to filter out the negative. I don't know how many times I have heard this. Go and sit down, woman, I will deal with you later.

Petya, while society paints the iris, we, poets, contemplate the beauty of the world. There is a magical reality in bird flight. Wisdom is the principle. I am a hard worker, trusting empirical formulas, and hope to encourage others with my message, like you, Petya. To hope. Into the river. Floating like scum. The sun is milking self-pity. Starlight and moon yonder square. War is not a temple although the battlefield of the mind is. The sea can take anything. Grace, you were a source of light. If darkness just had optimism. The telescope has a sacred heart like yours, Petya. Virgin, healing like an organ or tissue. Magic. Into the river. Then I think of the starlight and moon. Into the river. Anywhere but here.

www.ingramcontent.com/pod-product-compliance
Lightning Source LLC
LaVergne TN
LVHW051006080826
845145LV00009B/2482